Don't read this **Book**

蔡奕龍 作品

作者介紹：

蔡奕龍

1976年生

紐約大學Tisch藝術學院碩士。

旅居大蘋果五年。

擅長在洋基棒球球場對紅襪球迷嘶吼。

時常遇見耐人尋味的小事，因為怕別人不知道，而創作紐約‧台北《十二小時無時差》網誌。

28歲時因為一碗滷肉飯而返回台北。

目前任職於三立電視台，

兼任文化大學客座講師。

夢想是在曼哈坦買一間小房子。去紐約，也是回家。哈哈哈：D

catch 109　Don't Book 好個咚咚皮　蔡奕龍／著　責任編輯：韓秀玫　美術編輯：林家琪　法律顧問：全理律師事務所董安丹律師
出版者：大塊文化出版股份有限公司　台北市105南京東路四段25號11樓　讀者服務專線：0800-006689　TEL：(02)87123898　FAX：(02) 87123897
郵撥帳號：18955675　戶名：大塊文化出版股份有限公司　e-mail:locus@locuspublishing.com　**www.locuspublishing.com**
行政院新聞局局版北市業字第706號　版權所有　翻印必究
總經銷：大和書報圖書股份有限公司　地址：台北縣五股工業區五工五路2號　TEL：(02) 8990-2588（代表號）　FAX：(02) 2290-1658
初版一刷：2006年 4月　定價：新台幣220元　ISBN 986-7059-08-5　Printed in Taiwan

謹獻給我的父母
to my family

有了小孩之後，說Don't的機會就變多了。

Don't touch that, do that...

Don't put that in your mouth...

公司有規模了之後，說Don't的機會也變多了。

Don't compromise, stop...

Don't want to wipe your ass...

30 歲了，Don't 已成為一種本能，

Don't want to admit, but I am becoming my father.

奕龍的Don't述說：我們的經驗、無奈與妥協。

2.16.06

DEM Inc. Chairman/CEO Demos Chiang

橙果設計 執行長 蔣友柏

Life has its ups and downs, nooks and crannies, this book captures these little moments with a delicate application of dark humor which will keep you delighted for hours to come.   It will make you more aware of your surroundings and the consequences of your actions.

生活中多有起浮縫角，《Don't Book》以細膩的黑色幽默捕捉這些微妙片刻，帶給我們愉悅的閱讀時間，與一個簡單的生活態度。

2.16.06

DEM Inc. President/COO Edward Chiang
橙果設計 營運長 蔣友常

不要問我

不要問我發生了什麼事，
我一點都不想告訴你。

Don't Ask.

I know you are curious about my injury.
I am not gonna tell you what happened.
So, don't ask.

我可以告訴你為什麼我愛吃蘋果，..... 因為我喜歡紅色

我昨天晚上和誰出去玩，................ 隔壁鄰居 Pocha

我最欣賞的搖滾樂手，.................... 邦喬飛

甚至是我放棄彈鋼琴的秘密。......... 常常一邊彈著卻一邊睡著了 ^z^z^z

但是請不要問我發生了什麼事，....... 有關於繃帶的都不會是好事

我可是一點都不想告訴你。............. 一點都不想

別氣餒

不相信自己，至少相信機率吧。

Don't Be Disappointed

Believe in probability.

命中紅心只是遲早的事。
That very one shot will come eventually.

別有罪惡感

試一下就好，沒有關係啦！

Don't Be Guilty

It's no big deal, just give it a try.

別那樣做

那樣做是不對的！

Don't Do That

It is very wrong to do so.

別嫉妒
Don't Be Jealous

樹上有顆南瓜，手中有個氣球！

I see a pumpkin on the tree as I'm holding a balloon in my hand.

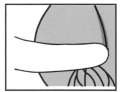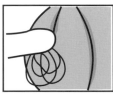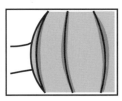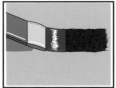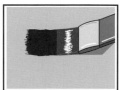

你也可以辦到！
You can make one, too.

早到吧

不過人可以等時間啊。

Be Early

But any man can wait for the time to come.

These horizontal lines are parallel, or not ?

圖中的每條水平線都相互平行，還是不然？

别相信你的眼睛
Don't Believe Your Eyes

Don't Be Nervous

Take a deep breath, you look great,
and yes, she does love roses.

別緊張

深呼吸，你看起來很體面，
而是的，她很喜歡玫瑰花。

別告訴我你忘了帶電影票。
Don't tell me you forgot the tickets.

別害怕

別摀著耳朵，
我可是練習了很久，
才會在這裡表演喔。

Don't Be Scared

Get your hands off your ears.
I have practiced a lot for this performance.

雖然我沒有馬友友一般的水準，但是你將聽到相同的熱情。

Although I don't n have Yo-Yo Ma's talent, you will hear the same passion.

別害羞
做自己！

Don't Be Shy
Be yourself.

洗髮精　　　　　　　水　　　　　　　　Api 的特製帽子

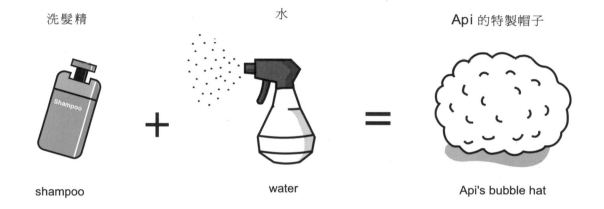

shampoo　　　　　　water　　　　　　Api's bubble hat

別太過分

喂！你過來。我已經注意你很久了。

Don't Be Too Over

You ! Come here.
I have been watching you for a long time.

去翻翻書，看看什麼叫做「運動精神」。
Go check out what "Sportsmanship" means at google.com.

老子可是齊天大聖，有七十二般變化、
手拿伸縮自如的金箍棒、腳踩觔斗雲，
一躍十萬八千里，識相的就別擋路。

別得意忘形
不知道當年是誰逃不出如來佛的手掌心？

Don't Bluff

Who was trapped in Buddha's palm hundreds
of years ago? You arrogant monkey.

Don't Call Me.

" The number you have dialed is not available right now,
   please leave a message after the tone . . . . "

別打電話給我

「您撥的號碼現在收不到訊號，請於嗶聲後留言 . . . . . . 」

要做大事的人
在乎的不是瑣碎的小事

Great people do great things.
Don't let those tiny little trifles bother you.

就是不介意
Don't Care

妳也知道，

人生就是這樣子啊。

有時讓妳開懷大笑，

有時卻又讓妳難過不已。

就別流淚了，

美麗的玫瑰，給美麗的妳。

Hey,

life has ups and downs,

happiness and tears.

Just don't cry,

a beautiful rose

for a beautiful lady.

別流淚了
美麗的玫瑰，給美麗的妳。

Don't Cry
A beautiful rose for a beautiful lady.

只有一個地球

如果每個人都能有一次機會，

只要一次，

能夠從暗黑的宇宙裏，

凝視自己所居住的，這顆柔弱美麗的行星，

大家的生命價值觀就會有很大的改變也說不定。

If everyone could have a chance,

just one chance,

to gaze at this delicate and beautiful planet

from the immense Universe,

maybe your value of life would change completely.

Only One Earth

別破壞她

地球只有一個，生命只有一次。

Don't Destroy It

There is only one Earth. There is only one lifetime.

Don't Disturb

Playing video games can be very serious.
So leave me alone, if you don't mind.

請勿打擾

打電動玩具是會很認真的，所以
如果沒什麼要緊事，請不要吵我。

忠於自己

做的。」印象

問題2 你希望A-pi能帶給人的

帶給那些我曾經在公車、路上

開懷的一笑。

由A-pi數層的表情，加

洩情緒與文字上

（d poet society）　3.百老

我的良師益

從愛迪

形

要活就要Don't

Don't Book

蔡亦龍作品

Don't Book

親情、勵志方面，對

問題5 喜歡旅行嗎？最喜
1.超級愛旅行，總是能在旅
物。
2.住經驗:紐約/旅行經驗:威尼斯

問題6 生命中無法承受之輕是？絕對無
西是？
我想應該是親情吧。無法缺少——愛情。

問題7 對你而言畫圖創作是什麼？
是我腦袋/心的麥克風，是通往世界與你/妳心理的
路。勾動你/妳靈魂的一根針。

問題8 你喜歡什麼風格的房子？如何佈置？
義大利式簡潔風格的房子是我很喜歡的樣子。
用亞曼尼或凱文克萊式的色調與簡單實用傢俱來佈置。

問題17 A-pi畫了多久？
2001年誕生開始斷斷續續一直到2005年間，有些短動畫的創作。正式開始針對書籍創作則是2004年開始。

問題18 下一本書的計畫是？
1.以A-pi創作另一本Be Book（Be cool, Be quiet, Be strong, Be my girl……）
2.關於勵志、愛情的插畫書，傳達簡單卻深列的意念。

支蘇活
備及華
米羅、
秀拉的
是有這種好
一代藝術家的創
也感受到其創意或感
激出靈感。可惜我對繪畫的技術本身，遺憾

't Book創作過程中最糊忘的事情是？
一學期)就以A-pi製作了一系列動畫。當時的
獨斯卡動畫獲得主BOB GREENBERG還曾突
的忠實迷。在創作期間也在言語上給我很大的

別平常穿
今天是萬聖節，奇裝異服的出門吧！

Don't Dress Normal

It's halloween! Dress up and go out.

別　酒醉　駕車
Don't Drink and Drive

別掉下來

我現在只想著這檔事。

Don't Drop

That's all I pray for now.

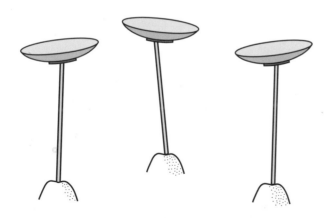

別吃太多

Don't Eat Too Much

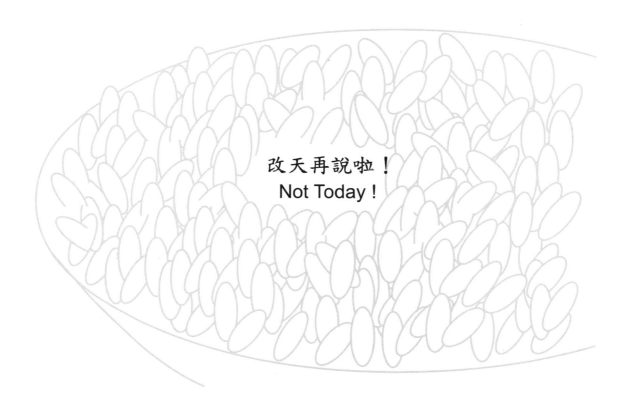

改天再說啦！
Not Today !

想都別想

就算是天塌下來我也不管。

Don't Even Think About It

Nothing can drag me out of my comfy blanket.

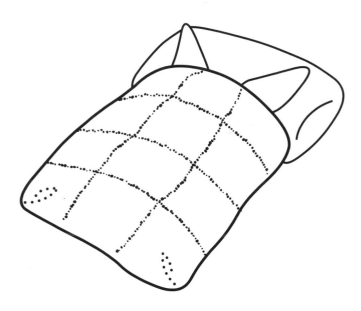

尤其在週六早上 . . . . .
Especially when it's Saturday morning . . . . .

別掉下去

走在危險的高空繩索上，
我的保險公司一定比我更緊張吧。

Don't Fall

Walking on a dangerous high wire,
I believe this is what my insurance company would say.

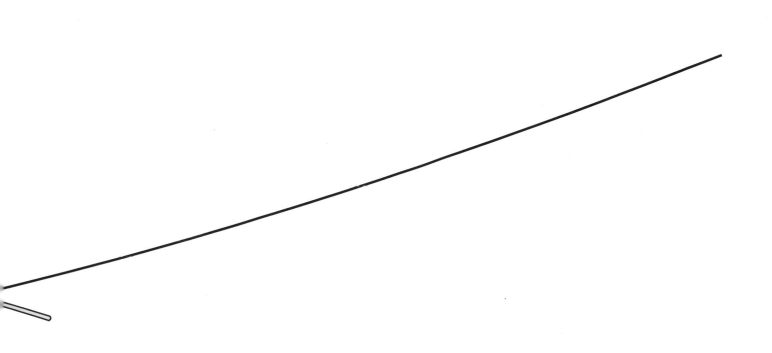

請平平穩穩地走出每一步　別擔心腳步太慢　反正人生本來就不長嘛

不讓你翻頁
Don't Flip the Page

Don't Fool Me

I am not a bad bad guy, but still,
don't fool with anyone who
has a stick in his mouth.

別想唬弄我

雖然我不是壞人，但是你也不要
惹嘴中刁著一根樹枝的人。

別忘了
Don't Forget.

10:00　NBA 季後賽直播 \ NBA Playoffs Live
14:00　下午茶時間 \ Afternoon Tea
16:00　購買日用雜物 \ Grocery Shopping
17:00　洗衣店拿衣服 \ Pick Up Laundry
19:00　瑜珈課 \ Yoga Class

生活中有那麼多「別忘了」的事情；

別忘了打卡，

別忘了帶雨傘，

別忘了關門，

別忘了繳費，

別忘了拿發票，

別忘了拔鑰匙……

即使把這些事情通通都忘掉，

妳的笑容應該還是一樣甜美吧！

Don't forget to check in,

to bring an unbrella,

to close the door,

the payment,

the reciept,

your keys.....

Even I forget all of these,

I still remember your smily face :)

不要忘記自己是誰
Don't Forget Who You Are

和當時的夢想與目標
and What You Have Always Wanted to Be

別 皺 眉
Don't Frown

"A day without laughter is a day wasted."   ~Charlie Chaplin

卓別林說：「每天都值得一個微笑。」

就是不在乎
Don't Give a Damn

Don't Give Me That Look

You asked it yourself.
You should pay for what you did.

別給我臉色看

這是你自找的。敢作要敢當！

不要放棄

如果你現在就放棄，你就永遠
不知道努力的結果是什麼了！

Don't Give Up

You'll never know what you are
going to get if you give up now.

偌大的世界在等著你
The world is out there.

別放棄

認輸永遠不會是我的選擇。

Don't Give Up

Giving up has never been a choice for me
and will never be one, either.

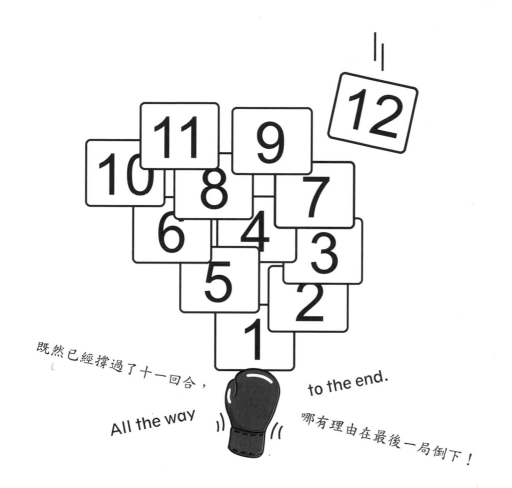

既然已經撐過了十一回合，

All the way to the end.

哪有理由在最後一局倒下！

73

別急著走

充電過程還未結束，
不要急，有耐心一點。

Don't Go

You are not fully charged yet.

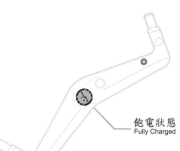

飽電狀態
Fully Charged

準備充分再出發吧

別自顧著走啊
等等我。

Don't Go by Yourself
Wait for me.

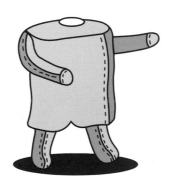

別走太遠

生病復原時，起來走走是件好事，
但也請不要運動過度。

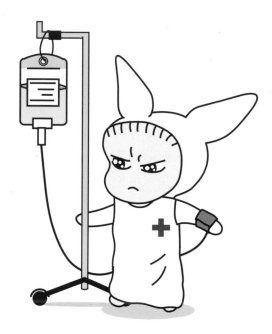

Don't Go Too Far

Take a short walk is good for recovery,
 but don't over exercise.

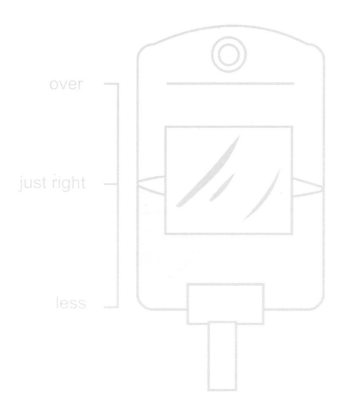

over

just right

less

許多時候，「剛剛好」的選擇，
就是最好的決定。

Most of the time, the best decision is to
make a ìjust rightî choice.

不要用猜的

這是視力檢查表，不是猜字遊戲，
看不清楚時就直說，眼見為憑。

Don't Guess

It's all for the good of your eyes, so if you can't
read it, just say you can't. To see is to believe.

許多事情是不需要靠運氣的。

坦然面對眼前的問題，

並做出誠實的選擇，

才是對自己最好的處理方式。

就從視力檢查開始練習吧！

我厭惡早起

我不喜歡肚子餓

我討厭收到帳單

我討厭插隊的人

我討厭看不見天空

我討厭菸味

我討厭不誠實的人

我討厭冷漠

不要心存恨意

你可以很容易說出一大堆憎恨世界的藉口，但是愛的理由只需一個。

我愛自己

我討厭蔬菜

我討厭加不完的班

我受不了塞車

我厭惡報紙的社會版

我討厭空氣污染

我討厭做作的人

我無法忍受髒亂

我討厭虛偽的人

Don't Hate

Surely you can find a whole bunch of
reasons to hate the world, but you
only need one to love. Love Api.

別猶豫
選擇一項運動，然後盡情的流汗吧！

Don't Heisitate
Pick a sport and burn up your energy.

別光顧著看

來幫忙啊！

Don't Just Look

Help!

別光說不練
Don't Just Talk the Talk

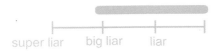

super liar　　big liar　　liar

不要說謊

記得「木偶奇遇記」嗎？
它告訴我們誠實時為上策。

Don't Lie

Do you know the Pinocchio fable?
It teaches us that honesty is the best policy.

不過，《綠野仙蹤》裡奧茲大法師的善意謊言，卻給予人無比的勇氣與信心。
But the white lies told by the Wizard of OZ, on the contrary, give people courage and hope.

別看我

是啦！我得了德國麻疹，
你看別的地方好不好。

Don't Look

Yes, I got German measles.
Could you please look away ?

終 身 保 固
Lifetime Warranty

一但感染德國麻疹，身體便自然產生抗體，

復原之後，再次感染的機率是零。

People who have had German measles once develop

a lifetime immunity

Don't Worry

People who have had German measles once
develop a lifetime immunity.

別擔心

生過一次德國麻疹，
就能終身免疫。

Don't Lose Focus

Left,

right,

left,

middle ......

別失神

左邊、

右邊、

左邊、

中間....

You are lucky !

算你運氣好！

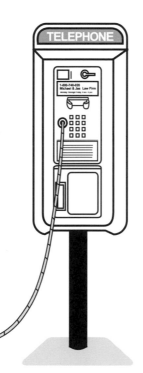

別逼我
時間就是金錢，請長話短說。

Don't Make Me
Time is money, so cut it short, please.

Don't Mess   With Me

Trust me, that's the   last thing you wanna do.

别惹我   相信我！那是你最不想做的事情。

Especially when I am hungry....
特別是當我肚子餓的時候 . . . . .

本期頭獎號碼：3 17　19 26 38　39
winning numbers

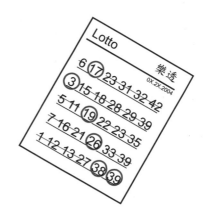

日	Today	Tomorrow	Monday	Tuesday	Wednesday
天氣	雨	雨	雨	多雲時晴	晴
氣溫(℃)	18°-24°	12°-18°	16°-22°	20°-25°	22°-28°
降雨機率	80%	60%	70%	N/A	N/A

別失誤啊

有些事情可以容許偏差，但是也有
許多事情是一點都不能出錯的。

Don't Miss

It's OK to miss the bus, miss the point,
miss the class.... But when it comes to
something like this, it's not OK at all.

別動

不然我怎麼好好幫你們拍照。

Don't Move

So that I can take a good photo of you.

別動

再等半小時就好了，
時間到之前別亂動啊！

Don't Move

It only takes half an hour for this treatment.
Please don't move during this time.

別說教了
考二十九分沒那麼糟糕吧。

Don't Preach
Come on, 29 is not that bad, take it easy.

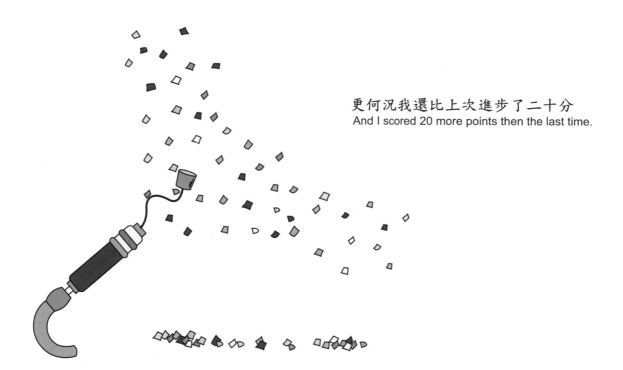

更何況我還比上次進步了二十分
And I scored 20 more points then the last time.

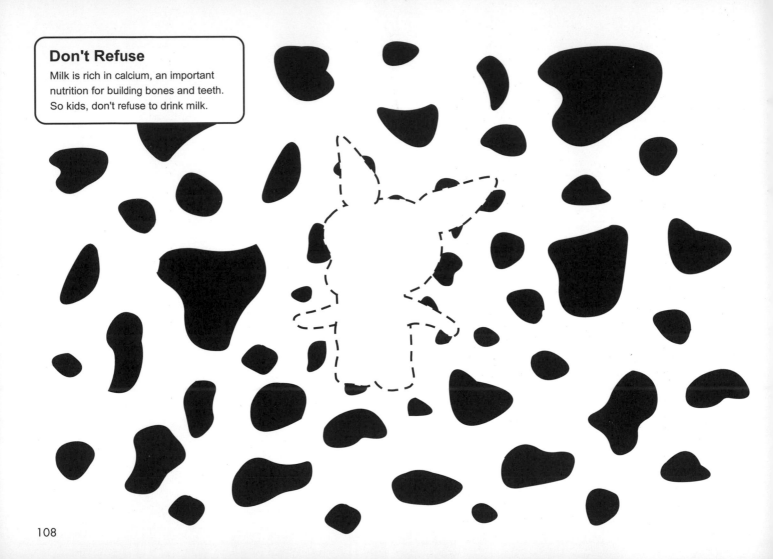

Don't Refuse

Milk is rich in calcium, an important nutrition for building bones and teeth. So kids, don't refuse to drink milk.

108

別拒絕

牛奶含有豐富的鈣質，而鈣質又是人
體骨頭和牙齒生長的重要營養素。
所以，小朋友們要多喝牛奶喔！

別拒絕

擁有我的愛情、我的生命、

Don't Refuse

I give you my love, my life,

110

和 我 的 音 樂
and my music.

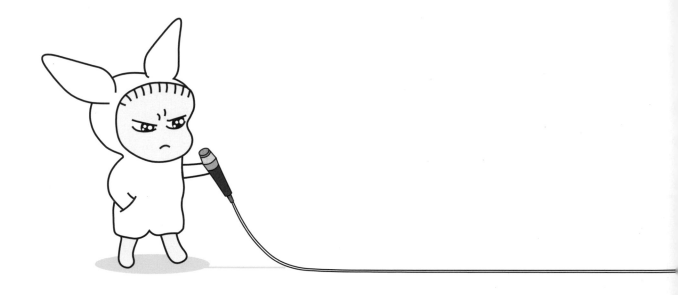

別逃跑

你們要跑到哪裡去！
給我的第一次卡拉OK表演一點支持嘛。

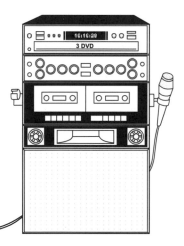

Don't Run Away

Come on, guys.
Show some support for my first Karaoke appearance.

別太匆忙

人生就像馬拉松一樣，
沒有什麼輸贏，
是過程重要還是結果重要，
你自己決定。

47th Central Park
MARATHON

Don't Rush :)

Life is like a marathon,
a game with no losers.
So whether the means justifies the
end or the end justifies the means,
you be the one to define it.

Don't Smoke

The overwhelming majority of lung cancers are caused by cigarette smoking. Lung cancer, the most preventable of all human cancers, remains the leading cause of cancer for both sexes.

別抽煙了

百分之九十的肺癌患者是因為吸煙造成。
而這全球死亡率第一的癌症卻也是最能
預防的癌症。

不要停

我不在乎你滾的多慢，
就這樣直直的向洞口前進吧！

Don't Stop

Keep going, I don't care how slow
you roll. In the hole!

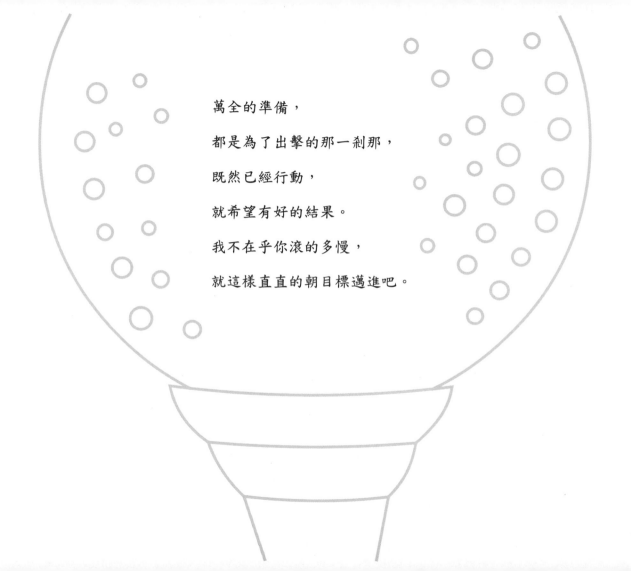

萬全的準備，

都是為了出擊的那一剎那，

既然已經行動，

就希望有好的結果。

我不在乎你滾的多慢，

就這樣直直的朝目標邁進吧。

別停

繼續嘩啦嘩啦的出來吧。
這是我的幸運日，只有在拉斯維加斯！

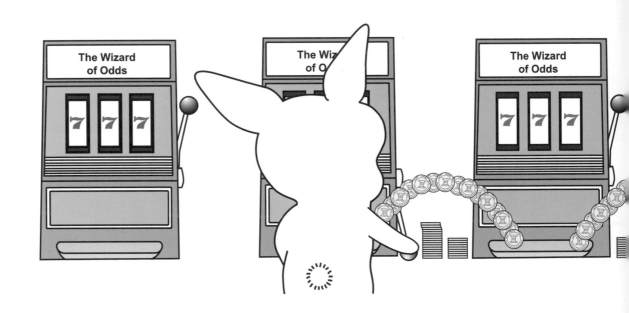

Don't Stop
Just keep coming out.
It's my lucky day, it's Las Vegas.

stays here.

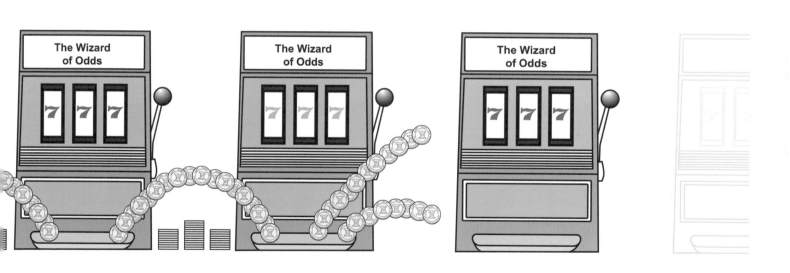

[1]

[2]

[3]

[4]

[5]

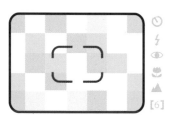

[6]

不要拍我

數位相機的全球普及率愈來愈高，
不管你拍什麼，就是不要拍我。

Don't Take My Picture

The popularity of digital cameras increases so fast.
Whatever you shoot, just don't take my picture.

Don't Think Before You Jump

Sometimes all you need is just ...... a lot of guts.

不要三思而後行

有時候你需要的只是....很大的勇氣。

請勿觸摸

事出必有因，就收起你的好奇心，把手收回去吧。

Don't Touch

Curiosity kills the cat.

別碰我的麵

世界上有數百種好吃的麵。去找你自己喜愛的口味，
不要理我和我的蔬菜湯麵。

Don't Touch My Noodles

There are hundreds kinds of noodles out there.
So go get yours, leave me and my noodles alone.

不要越線

我不想傷害你，但是當我必須出手時，
我是不會留情的。

Don't Trespass

I don't wanna hurt you, but if I have to,
I won't heisitate.

別關燈
Don't Turn Off the Light

喂！ #$*%&#

Don't Waste Your Wish

You can make a wish, any kind of wish.
But you have to say it in 5 seconds.
5 . . . 4 . . . 3 . . .

別浪費你的願望

你可以許一個願望，什麼願望都可以，
但是必須在五秒內說出來。
五 . . 四 . . . 三 . . . .

機會是給準備好的人

Always well prepare yourself,
the once in a lifetime chance doesn't make any reservation.

有時候，一句話的力量，可是大的驚人。

Sometimes simple words can be very powerful.

別擔心

這是一次極為成功的手術。

Don't Worry

Everything went really well.
It's a very successful surgery.

Don't You Agree ?

Jazz
Blues
Soul
Hip-hop
Funk
R&B
Salsa
Country
Pop
Classics
Reggae
Rock'n Roll
Heavy Metal
Rave
Electric
Trance
....

不同意嗎？

爵士
藍調
靈魂樂
嬉哈樂
放克
節奏藍調
騷沙樂
鄉村樂曲
流行樂
古典樂
雷鬼
搖滾樂
重金屬
銳舞
電子樂
全斯
....

No Music, No Life.

無 樂ㄩㄝˋ 無 樂ㄌㄜˋ

我愛

大的驚人
very powerful

141

不愛下雪嗎

我愛極了這天上落下的白色顏料。

Don't You Love Snow

I love it so much - the beautiful white color falling from the sky.

Each and every snowflake is unique.

You can't find two identical flakes, just like you can't find another you anywhere in the world.

Don't Doubt

別懷疑

天空落下的每個雪片都是獨一無二的結晶。

世界上沒有兩個一樣的雪片，

就如同世界上找不到另一個妳一樣。

請浪費生命

生命就應該浪費在美好的人事物上。

Do Waste Your Life

Life ought to be spent on beautiful things.

國家圖書館出版品預行編目資料

Don't book／蔡奕龍圖/文.--初版.--臺北
市：大塊文化，2006【民95】
面； 公分.--(catch；109)

ISBN 986-7059-08-5 (平裝)

855   95005211

大塊文化出版股份有限公司　收

姓名：

地址：□□□

　　　　　　　市／縣　　　鄉／鎮／市／區

路／街　　段　　巷　　弄　　號　　樓

編號：CA 109　書名：Don't Book

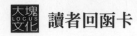 **讀者回函卡**

謝謝您購買這本書，爲了加強對您的服務，請您詳細塡寫本卡各欄，寄回大塊出版 (免附回郵) 即可不定期收到本公司最新的出版資訊。

姓名：＿＿＿＿＿＿＿＿＿＿＿＿　身分證字號：＿＿＿＿＿＿＿＿＿＿＿＿　性別：□男　□女

出生日期：＿＿＿年＿＿＿月＿＿＿日　聯絡電話：＿＿＿＿＿＿＿＿＿＿＿＿

住址：＿＿＿＿＿＿＿＿＿＿＿＿＿＿＿＿＿＿＿＿＿＿＿＿＿＿＿＿＿＿＿＿＿

E-mail：＿＿＿＿＿＿＿＿＿＿＿＿＿＿＿＿＿＿＿＿＿＿＿＿＿＿＿＿＿

學歷：1.□高中及高中以下　2.□專科與大學　3.□研究所以上

職業：1.□學生　2.□資訊業　3.□工　4.□商　5.□服務業　6.□軍警公教　7.□自由業及專業　8.□其他

您所購買的書名：＿＿＿＿＿＿＿＿＿＿＿＿＿＿＿＿＿＿＿＿＿＿＿

從何處得知本書：1.□書店 2.□網路 3.□大塊電子報 4.□報紙廣告 5.□雜誌　6.□新聞報導 7.□他人推薦 8.□廣播節目 9.□其他

您以何種方式購書：1.逛書店購書 □連鎖書店 □一般書店　2.□網路購書 3.□郵局劃撥 4.□其他

您購買過我們那些書系：

1.□touch系列　2.□mark系列　3.□smile系列　4.□catch系列　5.□幾米系列 6.□from系列　7.□to系列　8.□home系列　9.□KODIKO系列

10.□ACG系列 11.□TONE系列　12.□R系列　13.□GI系列　14.□together系列　15.□其他

您對本書的評價:(請塡代號 1.非常滿意　2.滿意　3.普通　4.不滿意　5.非常不滿意)

書名＿＿＿＿　內容＿＿＿＿　封面設計＿＿＿＿　版面編排＿＿＿＿　紙張質感＿＿＿＿

讀完本書後您覺得：1.□非常喜歡 2.□喜歡　3.□普通　4.□不喜歡　5.□非常不喜歡

對我們的建議：＿＿＿＿＿＿＿＿＿＿＿＿＿＿＿＿＿＿＿＿＿＿＿＿＿＿＿

＿＿＿＿＿＿＿＿＿＿＿＿＿＿＿＿＿＿＿＿＿＿＿＿＿＿＿＿＿＿＿＿＿＿＿

請沿虛線撕下後對折裝訂寄回，謝謝！